The Most Popular Girl
in School

"Who *is* Celia Forester, anyway?" asked Sonya.

"She's only the most popular girl in our grade. Maybe in the whole entire school," Angela replied.

"Why didn't you tell me about her?" Sonya asked. In all the letters, there had been no mention of Celia. And she looked like somebody who would be noticed.

Terri sniffed. "Ha! She wasn't worth writing about. Celia is a jerk. You should see the way she eats. She acts like she's afraid to get her teeth dirty."

Sonya didn't understand why her friends didn't like Celia. What was so bad about her? She felt left out because she didn't know. But she didn't think it would take her long to find out.

Books by Susan Smith

Samantha Slade #1: Samantha Slade: Monster Sitter
Samantha Slade #2: Confessions of a Teen-age Frog
Samantha Slade #3: Our Friend: Public Nuisance #1
Samantha Slade #4: The Terrors of Rock and Roll

Available from ARCHWAY Paperbacks

Best Friends #1: Sonya Begonia and the Eleventh Birthday Blues
Best Friends #2: Angela and the King-Size Crusade
Best Friends #3: Dawn Selby, Super Sleuth
Best Friends #4: Terri the Great
Best Friends #5: Sonya and the Chain Letter Gang
Best Friends #6: Angela and the Greatest Guy in the World

Available from MINSTREL Books

#1 Sonya Begonia
and the
Eleventh Birthday Blues

by
Susan Smith

A MINSTREL® BOOK

PUBLISHED BY POCKET BOOKS

New York   London   Toronto   Sydney   Tokyo   Singapore

A MINSTREL PAPERBACK *ORIGINAL*

A Minstrel Book published by
POCKET BOOKS, a division of Simon & Schuster Inc.
1230 Avenue of the Americas, New York, NY 10020

ISBN: 0-671-73033-9

First Minstrel Books printing April, 1988

10 9 8 7 6 5 4 3

BEST FRIENDS is a trademark of Susan Smith.

A MINSTREL BOOK and colophon are registered trademarks
of Simon & Schuster Inc.

Printed in the U.S.A.

Sonya Patton,
this book is for you.

Sonya Begonia
and the
Eleventh Birthday Blues

Chapter One

❀

Sonya Plummer walked through the halls of Gladstone Elementary School, looking for a friendly face. Being NEW was like having cooties. Kids weren't exactly friendly. They looked at you strangely, as if they were thinking, "Ick—who's that?"

Sonya wanted to explain to everybody that she wasn't really NEW. She had friends at Gladstone, from when she used to go to school here. Her friends, Terri, Dawn, and Angela, were supposed to meet her in front of the attendance office. But in the excitement of Sonya's return to Gladstone, the girls had forgotten to tell her where the office was located in the new building. Sonya had no idea where she was going.

A group of girls stood in the hallway talking. Sonya stepped over to the one who stood out in the crowd—a redhead. Summoning her courage, she tapped the girl on the shoulder. "Um, excuse me, where's the attendance office?"

"It's downstairs," the girl replied, pointing down a flight of steps and brushing her reddish-gold bangs off her forehead as if she wanted to get a better look at Sonya. She was very pretty, Sonya decided, and also very trendy. She was wearing a big bright green sweater, black pants, and socks with little green apples printed on them. Looking Sonya up and down, the girl asked, "Are you new here or something?"

The word made Sonya cringe. "Well, not really," she said. "I mean, sort of."

The girl gave Sonya a funny look. "Either you are or you aren't. And if you aren't, you must have amnesia. Otherwise you'd know where the attendance office is."

The other girls burst out laughing. Sonya thought she recognized them from when she used to go to the old school. That was two years ago, when she was in fourth grade. She wished she could think of something funny to say, but the redhead kept on talking.

"Maybe you *do* have amnesia. My sister just tried out for a soap opera—for the part of a girl who gets amnesia."

"Are you kidding, Celia?" one of her friends exclaimed.

"No, I swear. It's true."

Sonya decided she'd rather have amnesia than be new. She sighed. "I went to Gladstone Elementary two years ago, before it moved to this new building," she explained. "That was in my last life."

"Your last life?" The girl named Celia looked puzzled, but then she smiled as though she knew what Sonya was talking about. "Oh, well, that explains it. Your clothes, I mean."

Sonya blushed bright red and looked down so nobody

could see her turn into a tomato. Her brown hair fell across her face, helping to hide it from view. Then she noticed her short black boots. The other girls were wearing sneakers. Sonya could've worn sneakers, too. She should have remembered to ask Terri, Dawn, and Angela about clothes when they'd talked on the phone the night before. She'd forgotten how ultracasual everybody was in Gladstone. And Sonya, after her year in New York, looked like she was from somewhere else. She might as well have been wearing a badge that said NEW GIRL.

Seeing herself as they must see her, Sonya wanted to cry. She was a weird new person dressed in a mini-skirt with too many bracelets. Every time she moved she jingled, sounding as if she had a lot of change in her pockets.

"You don't look like you used to go to school here," said Celia. "You look like you're from Hollywood or someplace."

"Hollywood?" Sonya blinked in amazement. "Really? Well, I lived in New York."

"New York! New York *City?* Wow!" Admiration rippled through the small group. Celia smiled and said warmly, "I'm Celia Forester."

"I'm Sonya Plummer," Sonya replied, glad the fact that she'd lived in New York was such a hit.

"Oh, I remember you," exclaimed one of the girls, whom Sonya finally remembered was Jeannie Sandlin.

She also recalled that she and Angela used to sing, "I dream of Jeannie with the mouse-brown hair . . ." to describe Jeannie, whom neither of them had liked.

"You're Jeannie, right?" said Sonya.

"And you're Polly Clinker." Sonya remembered the other girl whose pinched face was hidden behind thick glasses. Without her glasses on, she always squinted fiercely. Both Jeannie and Polly had just been big blobs back in fourth grade. They would never stand out in a crowd—not like Celia. Sonya wondered why on earth the three of them were hanging around together. They didn't seem like they would be friends.

"Do you want to sit with me at lunch?" Celia asked suddenly.

"Well," answered Sonya, "I usually sit with my friends, but today . . . okay, thanks." She was pleased that she already had friends and was not really just a new kid. But she was also flattered that Celia had invited her to eat lunch.

"See ya," Celia said as she turned to leave, and Polly and Jeannie chimed in.

"See ya," replied Sonya. Her heart thudded loudly, blotting out the sounds of the other students as she ran down the stairs two at a time.

Sonya's return to Gladstone, California, had been unexpected. She'd been surprised when her father had asked her to come live with him in New York after fourth grade. But both her parents had thought it would be a good opportunity for her, while her mother was building her new career in another area. Then her mother remarried and wanted Sonya to move back to California to live with her. Sonya wasn't wild about her new stepfather, but she was sure that returning to Gladstone would be easier than starting out somewhere completely new.

Sonya was determined to fit in at Gladstone Elementary

quickly. However, she wanted to fit in and stand out at the same time. She figured it would be a good idea to make new friends, get involved in interesting projects, and be somebody important. She wanted sixth grade to be the best school year ever.

Sonya stopped at the attendance office to get her class schedule. Ms. Pring, who'd been the office secretary for years and years, was not there. A new lady with stiff blond hair stood behind the counter. So not only was Gladstone in a different building, but the faces had changed, Sonya realized. She took her schedule, noting that Ms. Bell would be both her homeroom and her English teacher. Sonya was not pleased. Ms. Bell was the teacher everyone wanted for fifth grade.

Sonya stood outside the office, wondering where her friends were. They were usually on time.

The four girls had been friends since kindergarten when Sonya had moved next door to Angela, soon after the Plummers' divorce. One day Angela had accidentally hit Sonya with a mud pie while Sonya was sitting on her porch. Sonya had cried, Angela had apologized, and Angela's mother had suggested that they make mud pies together. By the end of the day, there were enough pies for a banquet.

During fifth grade, while Sonya was in New York, she and her friends had kept in touch by exchanging weekly letters. But the night before school started, Angela, Terri, and Dawn had picked up the extensions at Terri's house, and all four friends had spoken on the phone together for the first time in a year.

"Sonya? Sonya, is that you?"

Sonya turned around. "Angela?" she cried.

Angela King looked almost exactly the same as she had looked in fourth grade. She was plump with dark hair and a smile that lit up her face. Sonya's worries dissolved as she and Angela flung themselves into each other's arms.

"You're really back!" Angela couldn't help giggling as she jumped up and down.

"I can't believe it!" Sonya exclaimed. "Wow, you don't know how good it is to see you!"

Over Angela's shoulder, Sonya caught sight of Dawn Selby and Terri Rivera. "Hey, is that Sonya Begonia?" Terri called, breaking into a run. It was useless to tell somebody like Terri not to run in the halls. Within seconds, she had hurled herself at Sonya and Angela. Then Dawn nudged her way in, and the four began shrieking and talking at once.

"Yeah, we're together again! Best friends, right, Sonya?"

"Right, Angie."

The four girls were only vaguely aware that people turned around to watch them.

"Sonya, you look so different, so grown up," Dawn said. "Doesn't she look grown up, Angela?"

"Yeah, she looks New Yorky. That's what it is. Sonya Begonia, you look like a city girl. And you're so skinny. You can borrow some of my fat. I give fat transplants."

"But do I look all right?" Sonya asked anxiously.

"Sure, you look great, just great." Dawn was always ready with a compliment.

"I hardly recognized you, honest," Terri said, giving her a hug. "As you can see, nothing and nobody changes much around here.'' She pirouetted over to the bank of lockers. Terri was a gymnast and never missed a chance to jump or twirl.

''Oh, I don't know about that, Terri,'' said Sonya. ''You guys all look different. Well, older anyway. And this *is* a new school.''

After all her experiences, Sonya thought she had probably changed more than her friends had, but she did notice that Angela looked heavier than usual, and Dawn had cut her hair short. Terri was taller, but otherwise she was still bouncy and ready to mouth off at the first opportunity.

''What classes are you in, Sonya?'' Dawn asked.

Everybody brought out their schedules to compare.

''Oh, good. We all have the same homeroom,'' Angela noted. ''And we're in gym together, too. Come on. This is going to be fun.''

''What happened to the Dats Club?'' Sonya asked as they walked to class. The Dats Club (D for Dawn, A for Angela, T for Terri, and S for Sonya) had been formed during fourth grade.

''The what? Oh, yeah.'' Terri snorted and looked embarrassed.

''Well, what happened to it?'' Sonya persisted. ''I asked you about it in my letters, but you never told me.''

''That's because we haven't done anything with it,'' Angela explained. ''After you left, it kind of fell apart. It was only the 'Dat Club' then.''

Sonya laughed. She felt happy as part of the group again,

and pleased that they had thought she was so necessary to the club.

"I'm glad we have homeroom and gym together," she said as they walked along. "It bugs me that nothing's the same."

"The cafeteria food is the same," Angela said. "Hot dogs and baked beans today."

Sonya giggled. "Do they still have mushburgers?" she asked, remembering the gross burgers served in the lunchroom. The sauce, lettuce, and meat were always mushed together as though somebody had sat on them.

Angela, the authority on all food, said, "Now we have Mushburger II—a much better one."

The girls turned a corner, looking for their homeroom, and Sonya glanced up and saw Celia again, surrounded by her friends.

"There she is," whispered Sonya.

"Who?" asked Terri.

"The girl I met when I first came in," Sonya replied, pointing her out.

"Oh, you mean Celia Forester." Angela wrinkled her nose. "I guess you wouldn't know her. She moved here last year."

At that moment, Celia caught sight of Sonya and motioned to her friends. "Oh, there's Sonya. Hi, Sonya!" Celia cocked her head to one side. The other girls cocked their heads, too.

"Oh, brother!" groaned Terri. "The clone sisters."

The first bell rang then, and Celia gave her hair a dramatic toss and marched into the classroom. Sonya, Dawn, Terri, and Angela stayed out in the hall until Celia was out of hearing.

"Who *is* Celia Forester, anyway?" asked Sonya.

"She's only the most popular girl in our grade. Maybe in the whole entire school," Angela replied. "And unfortunately, she seems to be in our homeroom."

"Why didn't you tell me about her?" Sonya asked. In the letters, there had been no mention of Celia. And she looked like somebody who would be noticed.

Terri sniffed. "Hah. She wasn't worth writing about. Celia is a jerk. She's conceited."

"Well, maybe she's got something to be conceited about," Sonya said.

"So do we—right, everybody?" Dawn said.

"Except that we're not stuck-up," Terri reminded the others. "There's a difference—I think."

"*I* think we should all get medals," suggested Angela.

The girls nodded in agreement. Sonya looked at her friends. She guessed they were remembering when the four of them were the best-liked girls in the school. She took a deep breath and announced, "Celia Forester asked me to eat lunch with her today."

Angela, Terri, and Dawn gasped in mortal horror. "She didn't!"

"She did," Sonya replied, and told them how she had met Celia that morning. "I said okay, but I usually eat lunch with my friends," she added.

"Does that mean we all have to eat together?" Angela wanted to know.

"You don't have to sit with us if you don't want to," Sonya

said, feeling disappointed. She'd thought they'd be excited, too.

"Have you seen the way Celia eats?" Terri asked, giggling. "She acts like she's afraid to get her teeth dirty."

"Come on," Dawn said, pulling Sonya by the sleeve. "We'll be late for class."

The others followed them into the classroom, grumbling about Celia Forester. Sonya didn't understand why her friends didn't like Celia. What was so bad about her? She felt left out because she didn't know. But she didn't think it would take her long to find out.

Chapter Two

⚏

"My mother says you should eat with people you like. That way you get good vibes and you *don't* get indigestion," Angela informed Sonya, Terri, and Dawn. She unwrapped her sandwich and took a big bite.

"Do nice people make the food taste better?" Sonya asked. Angela's mother was the food critic for a magazine called *Food Sense*. It was obvious where Angela had inherited her love of food.

"Oh, sure. Lots of things make it taste better. Music, lights, nice atmosphere."

Angela's mouth was full. Sonya hated listening to someone talk with her mouth full.

"I like cafeteria sounds," Dawn piped up dreamily. "Have you ever heard that *ping* that forks make when they hit the floor in here?"

"Dawn, *honestly,* who pays attention to stuff like that?" Terri asked. Abruptly, her expression changed. "Uh-oh, look who's coming."

Celia breezed through the cafeteria, carrying her tray which held only an orange and a carton of yogurt.

"Do you want to sit at my table?" she asked Sonya, ignoring the other girls.

"Why don't you sit here?" Sonya offered. "There's room." She patted the empty place next to her.

Celia sat down.

"Is that all you're eating?" asked Angela, staring over her double helping of chocolate pudding.

"Yes." Celia scooted toward the end of the table, so she looked as if she weren't *really* part of the group. "My sister Barbara—you know, the one who's on TV? Well, she said I should lose weight if I want to be on TV, too."

"You're going to be on TV?" asked Terri, Angela, and Dawn at the same time.

In all the excitement, Sonya sloshed hot chocolate down the front of her shirt. She barely noticed. "Are you going to be on the soap opera with your sister?" she asked.

"Barbara doesn't know if she has the part yet," Celia answered, "but if she gets it, she's going to get me on TV, too. Isn't that exciting?" Celia beamed at her audience.

"Tell everyone about your sister's part," said Sonya. "Tell them about the amnesia."

Celia described Barbara's role in the soap opera.

The girls nodded. No one had anything more to say, because nobody felt they had anything very exciting to add to the conversation. After all, who could compete with going on TV?

Instead, they watched Celia daintily peel her orange and divide it so that its segments looked like the petals of a flower. She ate carefully. No juice dribbled down her chin. No seeds shot across the table.

Sonya wished she could be so neat. She mopped at the brown stains on the front of her shirt.

"Barbara's doing commercials right now," Celia went on. "For Glitz Shampoo. Have you seen them?" She took mouse-sized bites of her yogurt.

"Oh, yeah, I've seen them!" Dawn cried excitedly.

Terri shot her a dirty look.

Celia looked at the clock. "I'd better get going. I have to talk to Ms. Bell." She slid on a jacket and stood up. "See you later, Sonya . . . everybody."

"Look how she walks," whispered Terri as Celia crossed the cafeteria. After Celia had passed through the double doors, Terri did an imitation of the walk, wiggling her hips and tossing her hair back. Angela giggled and tried it herself. She looked like a baby hippo.

"I like the way Celia walks," said Sonya.

Her friends frowned at her.

"Well, I *do*," she said stubbornly.

"I think it's gross," huffed Terri.

"And what's the big deal about having a sister in Hollywood?" Dawn added. "I have a brother in Milwaukee. He sells refrigerators."

Sonya stared at her in amazement. She decided not to in-form her that Milwaukee and refrigerators were not half as interesting as Hollywood and television.

"My chocolate pudding didn't taste as good as it usually does, and it's all Celia's fault," Angela complained. Then she eyed the remains of her friends' lunches. "Anyone want that piece of carrot cake?" she asked.

Sonya's next class was English, and she was pleased to see that Celia was in the class, too. However, they didn't get to sit as close together as Sonya would have liked. This was because Ms. Bell created a permanent seating arrangement.

Ms. Bell was a perfectionist. She had perfect teacher speech, perfect curls, and a perfectly straight frown line between her eyebrows. She also wanted perfectly straight desk rows, arranged in boy-girl pairs. Sonya found herself seated next to Howard Tarter, the funniest boy in school. Celia sat directly across the aisle from her, though, so that wasn't too bad. She did wish that Angela, Dawn, and Terri were in the class, too.

Ms. Bell assigned an essay entitled "What I Did On My Summer Vacation"—a teacher favorite.

"Was there ever a teacher who *didn't* assign this essay?" complained Terri later when they were sitting cross-legged on the blue carpet in Sonya's bedroom. Every English teacher in the sixth grade had assigned it that night.

"You'd think they'd come up with something more original since they've had a whole summer to think about it," Sonya said. She opened a bottle of soda and poured some into paper cups for herself and her three friends.

Sonya's bedroom was painted pale yellow. She hadn't put

up posters because she hadn't been in the room very long and she wanted to think for a while about how she would decorate it. Before her mom had remarried and moved to the ranch house, Sonya had had a small room which she hadn't paid much attention to. But she wanted her new room to be perfect. So far, she had chosen a blue and yellow flowered bedspread and curtains. She had arranged photos of her family and friends on the dresser. Over her bed hung a collage she had made herself. It was composed of headlines from newspapers such as *The National Weekly News,* which read, "Ape Mom Steals Human Baby," "I Gave Birth to 17 Rabbits," and "I Married A Horse." A big wicker rocking chair sat in one corner of the room.

"What did I do this summer?" Dawn asked herself. "I spent it with my head in an oven." Dawn's parents owned a bakery and Dawn sometimes worked there when school was out.

"I perfected the cartwheel," said Terri, sprawling out full length on the carpet.

"I went to a couple of five-star restaurants," said Angela.

"I went to camp." It seemed like ages ago that Sonya had gone to summer camp. When it had ended and she had gone home to New York—just a couple of weeks ago—her father and mother had told her that she was moving to California to live with her mother. Then her mother had gotten remarried. This would have been fine except that she had married Cowboy Bob Stretch, the creepiest guy ever. And now they lived on a ranch instead of in town like they used to. The ranch was about a ten-minute bike ride from Gladstone.

The girls talked about summer for a while, then wrote their essays. When they had finished their homework, Sonya showed her friends around the ranch.

"I love this place," exclaimed Terri, climbing onto the corral fence. "I always wanted to live on a ranch."

Dawn fed one of the horses a potato chip.

"I never thought about ranch life until we moved here," said Sonya. "I feel so far away from everything."

"It's just like one of those big places on TV," said Dawn. "Like Dallas, where glamorous people ride around on horses."

"And in sports cars," Angela reminded her.

"Speaking of TV. Does anyone want to watch Celia's sister?" Sonya asked.

"No!" shouted her friends.

"Why not?"

"We don't care about Celia *or* her stupid sister," Angela replied crossly.

Sonya took a deep breath. "Well, I think Celia wants to be my friend, and I can't figure out why you act like she's some disease."

Terri turned to her and said seriously, "Sonya, you just got here. You don't know how nasty Celia really is. Believe me, she isn't somebody you want to be friends with."

After the others had left, Sonya turned on the TV. She sat in front of it for an hour, switching channels constantly in order to find Barbara's commercial. But it wasn't on. Or else Sonya kept missing it. Finally she went into her room and stood in front of the full-length mirror. She tried to walk the way Celia walked. She stuck her hips out and practiced flipping her hair around. Then she swung her shoulders back and forth. She looked a little weird, but Sonya figured these things took time.

After all, practice makes perfect.

Chapter Three

⚘

Sonya decided that she wanted Celia to think she was an exciting and wonderful person. She wanted her friends to think so, too, but she figured they already knew her, so there was no point in trying to impress them. Besides, Celia was different from Dawn, Terri, and Angela, or anyone else at school. She dared to be different. She had flair. She had style. Sonya liked that.

The next morning, Celia sought out Sonya in school.

"Oh, Sonya, you're just the person I wanted to see!" she cried, her eyes shining.

Sonya grinned. That was nice to hear.

"I *had* to watch for Barb's commercial on TV last night—you know how important that is," Celia said breathlessly.

"Oh, sure." More important than anything I have to do, thought Sonya.

18

"Well, I didn't get my homework done because of it. I spent two and a half hours looking for the commercial. So I was wondering if I could copy those math problems Mr. Sutter assigned." She straightened her apricot-colored T-shirt, which she was wearing with tight jeans.

"Sure," Sonya said, and she propped her knee against the wall and snapped open her binder. She would do the same for her other friends, so why not for Celia?

"You're a lifesaver," said Celia, clutching the homework papers to her chest.

Sonya smiled, feeling like the wonderful person that she really was.

A few minutes later, while Sonya was standing with her friends, Celia sailed over to return the borrowed homework.

"I don't know what I would've done without you," she said. Then she smiled and sauntered off down the hall.

"What was all that about?" Terri asked, watching Celia's red head disappear down a flight of stairs.

"Celia had to watch TV all night, so she couldn't do her homework," Sonya explained to her friends.

"What kind of an excuse is that?" exclaimed Dawn.

Angela shook her head. "I wonder what my mother would do if *I* used that excuse."

"Make you eat dog food," said Terri.

"It sure beats doing homework," said Sonya suddenly. "Imagine being on TV and getting all that attention."

"I hear you have to get up really early in the morning to go to the studio and then you have to stay up late reading

lines. I bet being on TV is worse than doing homework,''
Dawn said.

"Well, *I* heard that models have to rub Vaseline on their
teeth to keep them from sticking to their lips, because they
have to smile so much,'' said Angela.

"So the job has smile dangers.'' Sonya giggled. "Just
think, Barbara must have slimy kisses.''

"And a fake smile,'' Terri pointed out. "How could you
trust anybody who smiles for a living?''

That afternoon, Sonya went home and wrote a list. She
often wrote lists. She found them very helpful. This one was
a list of things she liked about Celia.

1. Looks
2. Clothes
3. Walk
4. TV Sister—or Connections

The last one bothered her deeply. Now why couldn't Sonya
be related to a star? Instead, she was related to a real-estate
broker (her mother) and a businessman (her father). The only
real-estate brokers who got on TV were the ones selling land
out in the middle of nowhere. "Beautiful Cheshire Mountain
property with lakeside view . . .''

According to her mother, the lake almost always turned out
to be a swamp, and there was usually no road and no place
to build a house.

Her father, an executive for a food company, never went
on TV, except once when somebody nearly died of food poi-

soning from eating Chippy Chips. He had to defend the company, but the potato chips were taken off the market anyway.

Sonya wondered about Cowboy Bob. She doubted that he'd ever been on TV. He'd probably break the screen.

Sonya's mother fixed spareribs for dinner that night. Bob made a big production out of cooking them on the barbecue. You'd think, thought Sonya, that he was the first person ever to barbecue ribs.

"Ever been on TV?" Sonya asked him casually, watching him tending the meat.

"Oh, Bob's been on TV, haven't you, honey?" her mom interrupted.

Sonya noticed that her mother was wearing a new fringed shirt and tight jeans. What happened to the old mom who used to love to get dressed up in silk shirts and businesslike suits?

"Yep. I was a bronc rider in the state rodeo," said Bob, smothering the meat with his special sauce.

"Oh, yeah? You rode broncs?" Sonya asked. She wasn't really impressed. Riding broncs was pretty stupid. You could get killed doing that. You could get squashed into hamburger meat.

"Why, sure. Had to give it up, though. Bad for my back." Bob leaned backward, his big stomach straining the buttons of his plaid Western shirt. Then he moved some of the ribs onto a platter and walked bowlegged into the house.

Sonya thought he looked a little (but just a *little*) like a TV star named John Caige, a blond, round-faced cowboy. John had a part on *The Whitneys,* a series about a Southern family, and played Beau Whitney, one of the good guys.

On Friday, at the end of the first week of school, Angela came over to spend the night with Sonya. The girls watched *The Whitneys* while Sonya's mother and Bob were out.

"Have you ever noticed how the bad guys on this show have the worst accents?" Sonya asked.

"Yeah," replied Angela. "The nice people have nice accents. They make you wish you were from the South. You can hardly understand the bad guys."

"Bob Stretch was on TV once." Sonya told Angela about the bronc riding.

Angela laughed. "No wonder he's so bowlegged."

When *The Whitneys* was over, Sonya and Angela made brownies and ate half of them. Later, Sonya's mom and Bob came in, all smiles, and ate a couple of brownies themselves before going to their room.

"Your mom looks different," Angela said after the adults left.

"Yeah, I think she had a lobotomy while I was in New York," said Sonya. "She's turned into a cowgirl."

"What's a 'lobotomy'?" asked Angela.

"It's when doctors sever these nerves in your brain to make you change," Sonya explained. "They've tried it out on murderers, I think, but they aren't allowed to do it to just anyone."

"Oh. Well, your mom isn't *that* different," said Angela.

"Parents just go crazy sometimes. They're not very realistic."

"*Your* mom's okay," Sonya said.

Angela shrugged and stuffed a brownie in her mouth. "All she can think of is food. It's always, 'Well, how do you like the hollandaise, Angela?' or 'Maybe we should have put more cheese in the pesto.' "

Angela did a great imitation of her mother, but Sonya didn't say anything. She was thinking that Angela and her mother were just alike. All Angela ever talked about was food.

Sonya was glad she wasn't anything like her own mother.

Chapter Four

One thing that Sonya and Celia had in common was an interest in clothes. That was something that Dawn, Terri, and Angela didn't care much about. Terri wore nothing but sweats and Angela thought she was too heavy to look good in anything. Dawn was the worst. She wore babyish clothes, such as turtlenecks with cats or dogs all over them. They were clothes you could tell her mother had picked out for her. But Celia had taste, and Sonya liked that.

On Monday, Sonya carefully chose a blue shirt, stone-washed jeans, and high-top sneakers, an outfit she was sure would fit in at Gladstone Elementary.

"Special occasion today, Sonya B?" asked her mother.

"Not really," Sonya answered, gulping down her cereal.

"You're lookin' like a rose in a cornfield, honey," said Bob, grinning.

24

Sonya managed a smile. "Thanks. I'd rather be a rose than an ear of corn any day."

"She's bloomed, don't you think, Bob?" her mother asked. "Just like a begonia."

"Never saw her before this fall, Nellie, so how am I to know? But she looks good." Bob nodded approvingly. "Real chic."

Sonya looked across the table at her stepfather, surprised that he even knew the word "chic." He was leaning against a kitchen counter with a toothpick between his teeth. Most of the time he walked around the ranch with straw hanging out of his mouth, as if he were a horse.

Sonya and Celia had wound up in almost every class together. Their science teacher, Mrs. Emmons, was their least favorite teacher. She was about three hundred years old, and had absolutely no sense of humor.

During science class that Monday, Mrs. Emmons ripped open a bag of colored balloons, which caused a stir among the students.

"No, we're not having a party, class," she announced quickly.

Everyone groaned.

"But we are going to blow up these balloons," she continued.

The experiment: Mix together equal parts of vinegar and baking soda in a bottle. Put a balloon over the mouth of the bottle and secure it with a rubber band. Then shake the bottle, and the mixture should create a gas which blows up the balloon.

"Sonya, be my partner," Celia said. She crinkled up her nose as Mrs. Emmons opened the vinegar.

"Okay." Sonya grabbed a handful of balloons in her favorite colors, blue and red.

"I'm wearing something new of Barbara's and I don't want to spill anything on it," Celia went on.

"So you want me to do the experiment?" Sonya asked. She had already stuck her spoon in the baking soda. "I'm wearing something old, but Mom won't be happy if I ruin it."

"Oh, you won't, Sonya," Celia replied. "Really. Just be careful."

If ketchup was dripping out of a hot dog, it landed on Sonya's T-shirt. If she stood on a street corner in a new coat, a car would come by and splash her with mud. Sonya was a mess looking for a place to happen. So she wasn't surprised when she sloshed vinegar on her blue shirt as she poured it into the bottle. She dabbed at it with a paper towel, then spooned some baking soda into the bottle, put a balloon over the top and wound a rubber band around the neck of the bottle.

Celia stood a safe distance away while Sonya shook the bottle. The gas formed. The balloon blew up beautifully.

And then it popped. Everyone in the class turned around to look at Sonya.

Sonya blushed, but Celia clapped her hands together. "Oh, look! We did it!" she exclaimed.

Mrs. Emmons made her way to Celia. "What a perfect example, Celia!" she exclaimed. "Class, did you see that?"

The class murmured appreciatively.

But when Terri heard the story at lunch that day she grumbled, "Celia got all the credit, and you ended up smelling like a pickle. Why did you let her get away with it, Sonya?"

"It's no big deal, Terri," Sonya replied, but it irked her. And she wished Terri would just shut up.

"She's the teacher's pet," said Angela. "Why do all teachers fall for that dopey phoney way of hers?"

Celia passed by their table just then. "Wasn't science class fun?" she asked Sonya breathlessly. Dawn and Terri exchanged looks. Celia leaned down to Sonya, lowered her voice and said, "Sonya, how about coming to my house to watch TV after school? We can look for Barbara."

"Sure!" replied Sonya. She was getting tired of listening to her friends carry on about Celia. And she was pleased with the invitation.

As soon as Celia left, Terri glared at Sonya. "You're going over to *her* house?"

"Yeah," Sonya said defensively. "So what?"

"Well, *I* think it's exciting," exclaimed Dawn. "None of *us* has ever been to Celia Forester's house before."

Terri transferred her glare to Dawn. "Who'd want to?" she asked.

"I've got an idea!" cried Angela. "Sonya, why don't you be our spy?"

"Spy? Why? What do you want to know?" Sonya asked.

"How can you ask that question?" cried Terri. "She's just

not a very nice person, that's all. Today she took all the credit for your experiment. And when she came to Gladstone last year, she took over! She acted like she was the queen of the whole school! We know more about her than you do.

"If you want to know what I think—I think she's the most awful person who ever walked the face of the earth."

Angela and Dawn nodded in agreement, but Sonya turned away in disgust. However, she agreed to spy a little on Celia. After all, Terri, Dawn, and Angela were her best friends. Maybe they knew what they were talking about. And they *had* known Celia longer.

Sonya soon learned that she was not cut out to be a spy, even though she arrived at Celia's house concentrating on being a really good one in order to please her friends. She was ready to notice every little flaw. But once she got inside Celia's door, she forgot all about being a spy. Celia's mother had just baked cookies for them. And everything in the house was perfect. There were glass tabletops and luscious thick carpets and modern chairs that looked too nice to sit in. After two minutes in the house, Sonya couldn't imagine Celia living anywhere else. And she couldn't concentrate on anything except not making a mess.

Sonya was careful not to drop crumbs on the fur rug in Celia's lush pink and white bedroom. In fact, she was sort of afraid to eat anything. She was sure that Celia never dropped food or spilled drinks. Celia always looked neat.

"Are you watching Barb's commercial, honey?" Mrs. Forester called from the living room.

"Yes, Mom," Celia called back dutifully. Then she turned to Sonya. "My mom wants me to be exactly like my sister. She thinks if I watch her enough, I'll be like her. Tell me what you think."

Celia turned on the TV and switched channels until she found the end of an afternoon soap opera. Barbara's face flashed onscreen. It was a perfect face—all-American looks, shiny blond hair, green eyes, white, even teeth.

"Oh, look! This is a new commercial, and she's got glitter in her hair!" cried Celia. "Don't you think I'd look good with glitter in my hair?"

Celia swung her head so that her thick red hair fanned out.

"Sure," Sonya said. Celia would look good with mud in her hair.

"Your hair will shine and shimmer, if you use Glitz Shampoo," the announcer insisted as Barbara whirled around, her hair filling the screen with blondness.

"I think you look just as good as your sister," Sonya told her.

"Really?" Celia asked. Then her face clouded over. "Well, too bad my mom doesn't think so." She sighed. "That's what I like about you, Sonya. You see what's good in people."

Sonya was pleased that Celia thought that. She decided it must be hard to be compared to an older, glamorous sister. There were times—and this was one of them—when Sonya was glad she was an only child.

When the girls had watched the commercial four times, Celia showed Sonya how to make a tinfoil cap for her head so that her hair wouldn't be full of static electricity. They

walked around Celia's bedroom like a couple of space crea-
tures for half an hour, waiting for results.

Celia took her cap off and examined it critically. "I'm not
so sure this does what it's supposed to," she said.

"I think it's fun anyway," Sonya exclaimed. She added
antennae by poking the eraser ends of two pencils into the
tinfoil.

Then Celia went to the refrigerator and took out a cucumber. She sliced off four pieces and handed two to Sonya. "My
mother puts these on her eyelids to make the swelling go away
when she has tired eyes."

"I've never had tired eyes," Sonya admitted, but she put
the cucumber slices in place. "How long do I leave them
on?" she asked, groping her way down the hall.

Celia started laughing. "Oh, about ten days!"

"Or until they start to smell, right?" Sonya added, still
holding the slices on her eyelids. She bumped into the door-
way to Celia's room and burst into giggles.

"I think you're supposed to sit down, Sonya," Celia said.
"You're going to kill yourself."

Those people who knew Sonya well knew that once she
started giggling hysterically, she couldn't stop.

"I'm going to take those cucumbers away from you before
you hurt yourself," Celia said, giggling too.

Sonya started thinking of headlines for *The National Weekly
News*. "Hey!" she exclaimed. "Get this. 'Killer Cucumber
Slices Found on Victim's Eyes.' "

Celia couldn't stop giggling either. "Where do you *get* these
ideas?" she asked.

Sonya just shook her head, pleased that she was such a big hit.

Later, she biked home and washed her hair, using some of her mother's expensive French creme rinse. She tried whirling around the room to see if her hair would fan out like Barbara's. But her hair was shorter, not blond, and had a mind of its own. It just looked messy.

Still, if she closed her eyes, she felt like Barbara. Or Celia. She wasn't sure which one, but she felt glamorous. Sonya started a new list.

1. Grow hair.
2. Buy Glitz Shampoo.
3. Be neat, or:
4. Don't eat.

Chapter Five

❀

"Guess what?" Dawn greeted her three friends in front of the lockers the next morning.

"What?" said Sonya, Terri, and Angela.

"I couldn't wait for you guys to get here," she said breathlessly. "Celia Forester has glitter in her hair."

"So what?" replied Terri.

"I think we should do something," said Dawn. "All the boys are betting on who'll be the first to get a piece of glitter from her hair."

"That *is* terrible," said Angela, whistling through her teeth. "She already gets more attention than she should. It's a crime."

"Where'd she get the idea to use glitter?" Dawn wanted to know.

"From her sister Barbara," Sonya answered knowingly. All eyes turned to her.

"Oh?"

"Barbara's commercial. I saw it four times yesterday at Celia's house. She had glitter in her hair, for Glitz Shampoo," Sonya explained.

"Tell us about the house," said Dawn.

Sonya described the fancy house and the pink and white room and how neat everything was. Terri scowled.

Angela frowned. "There must be something bad about her," she said. "She can't be perfect. Are you sure there's nothing else?"

"Nothing," Sonya said. "Not one thing."

In English class that day, Sonya plunked herself down across the aisle from Celia. Celia was wearing a pretty pink sweatsuit which looked like it had never been sweated in. The glitter flashed in her hair.

Celia read her summer vacation essay in front of the class. The subject: auditioning for a part in a commercial in Hollywood.

"Can you imagine that, class?" Ms. Bell oozed. "Our own Celia Forester in an audition."

"I think I'm going to barf," someone whispered.

"Your sister Barbara is on television now, Celia," Ms. Bell said. "Is that right?"

"Yes, she's the Glitz Shampoo girl," Celia announced proudly. She went on about Barbara, tossing her own red hair so that the overhead lights flashed on the tiny squares of glitter.

Sonya watched her, then looked down at her own essay. It

seemed plain in comparison. Boring, actually, but there wasn't time to change it. Needless to say, Ms. Bell called on Sonya next.

She stood up. "I went to camp this summer in the Berkshire Mountains of Massachusetts," she began. "The camp was on a lake and there was a lot of wildlife. We saw woodchucks, deer, otter . . ."

Sonya was just thinking how babyish her composition sounded, when Howard Tarter made a loud chuck-a-chuck noise.

Ms. Bell frowned at him. "Howard, please. I do not appreciate animalistic noises in my class."

Animalistic! The class nearly died of laughter. Sonya bumbled her way through the rest of her essay, but every time she caught Howard's eye, she wanted to laugh. Next, Jeannie Sandlin read her composition about swimming lessons, and then it was Howard's turn to read.

He stood up and dragged a big shopping bag to the front of the class. "Well, as some of you already know, I've been in Africa on safari with my parents the past two summers," he said. "These are some of the things I brought back with me." He proceeded to pull statues out of the bag—wooden statues of naked people. Everyone gasped, and Ms. Bell blushed to the roots of her hair.

"Uh, Howard, I'm sure those are very valuable and that your family doesn't want them broken," Ms. Bell said nervously. "After everyone has seen them, would you put them back in the bag, please?"

The class giggled. Sonya was glad Howard had just come

back from Africa. She had liked him a lot in fourth grade. And it was nice to have somebody in the class who was sort of new like herself.

When English class was over, the boys crowded around Celia. Howard stood next to Sonya, watching them. "A native ritual," he commented. "I like to observe things. This is like watching natives dance. Or chimps pick lice off each other."

Somehow, when Howard said something seriously, it made Sonya laugh. "Howard, you're weird," she said.

"I know a chimp when I see one," he said without smiling.

Africa had changed Howard, Sonya decided. He said and did strange and wonderful things. She watched him walk away.

Sonya met her friends in the lunchroom and they stood on line behind Celia and the admiring boys. Jeannie Sandlin and Polly Clinker hung around the fringes of the group, listening.

"Just look that way, Celia," said Eddie Martin. "Watch the Jell-O wiggle."

Dawn rolled her eyes and nudged Eddie, whom she kind of liked. "Jell-O doesn't wiggle unless you wiggle it," she said.

Celia giggled, and Dawn glowered at her. Celia tipped her face toward the dishes of Jell-O on the counter. Eddie reached over and tried to pick a piece of glitter from her hair.

"Ouch!" she squealed. "Eddie, you're pulling my hair!"

"But I got the glitter!" he announced proudly. He held it up—and it slipped out of his fingers.

"You dropped it, stupid," said Terri.

"That doesn't count, Eddie. You tricked me," said Celia. She flounced off to her seat.

Sonya and her friends, Celia and her friends, Eddie and two other boys all sat together, scrunched up at one table.

Dawn became very quiet. While nobody was looking at her, she pulled the end off of her straw wrapper and dreamily blew it across the table. It landed in Celia's hair.

Terri yelled, "Straw fight!" and everybody grabbed handfuls of straws and blew the wrappers around the room until the lunch monitor told them to stop.

Sonya was laughing so hard she thought she'd die, but Celia got up from the table and acted as if she didn't know anyone. Sonya gulped back her hysterics, watching to see where Celia was going. Then she followed her.

"I don't want to eat with Terri anymore," announced Celia.

"Why not? Everybody was just having fun," Sonya said defensively. "Didn't you have fun?"

Celia shrugged. "Not exactly. Blowing straw papers is not a very mature thing to do."

Sonya hadn't thought about that. She wondered if putting tinfoil on your head was more mature.

Celia kept talking. "You know, your friends are jealous of you. You're much more mature than they are."

"I am?" Sonya blinked in surprise. But she was secretly pleased. "Yeah, well, maybe I am."

On Saturday, Sonya biked to the mall with her friends. They looked at the record store, the clothing stores, and at posters. Sonya bought a poster of the ocean. Then they ordered milkshakes and pizza in a fast food place that was decorated in orange, pink, and brown. Angela finished her pizza, drained her milkshake, then asked Sonya, "Are you eating your crusts?"

Sonya handed her the leftover crust. No wonder Angela looked like a blimp, she thought.

The girls found a dime store and Terri bought a birthday card for her cousin. Dawn picked out a tiny stuffed bear which she named Pooky. She was a real nut over stuffed animals.

"We finished playing with Barbie dolls last year," said Terri.

"*I* still play with them," Dawn replied, hugging the bear to her chest as though somebody were going to snatch it from her.

"I gave up playing with my Barbie when her leg fell off in the middle of a gymnastics routine," said Terri. "Then I threw her in the garbage."

"Pooky says you're a doll abuser," Dawn informed her.

"Pooky can't talk, Goonhead," Terri retorted. Then she pointed at some brown spots on Pooky's face. "And besides, he's got cooties."

"He does not." Just to make sure, Dawn studied Pooky's face, then stuffed him in her pocket.

Terri couldn't resist one more comment. "Does so," she said.

Dawn's features scrunched up as though she had just bitten into a lemon. She started to cry.

"Oh, no, Terri, now you've turned on the faucet," Angela groaned. "We'll never get her to stop."

A saleswoman marched over to the girls. Sonya looked the other way, hoping no one would know she was part of this group.

"Girls, you're creating a scene," said the woman. "Will you please go outside the store to finish your argument?"

"It's not an argument," Terri insisted as the salesclerk ushered them out of the store.

"Young lady, I don't want to argue with you over whether it's an argument," the salesclerk said hotly.

Sonya wanted to crawl through the floor. The word "immature" flashed across her brain in big red letters. She concentrated on calming Dawn down. Then the girls went to an art store, where Angela wanted to buy some poster board. On impulse, Sonya bought some gold glitter, remembering how it had looked in Celia's hair.

"You're copying Celia," chanted Angela.

"I am not," Sonya returned, but she felt her face grow hot.

"Copycat," chimed in Terri.

"I just wanted to see what it would be like." Sonya checked her allowance. She had a dollar fifty in her pocket. She didn't want her friends to think she was a complete copycat, so she said, "I'm going to buy glitter in different colors so we can fool around with it."

"Great idea!" Dawn said.

The girls picked out red, blue, and green glitter.

But Sonya had misread the price tags. The glitter cost seventy cents, not fifty. The saleswoman had already rung up the purchase. Sonya needed sixty cents more for the three tubes, and her friends didn't have it.

Suddenly Angela realized what had happened. She grabbed the green glitter and started to take it back, but she bumped into a display and dropped the tube. Glitter spilled onto the floor. Someone stepped in it and tracked it to the back of the store.

"You'll have to pay for that, young lady!" cried the saleswoman.

Angela glanced around fearfully, then grabbed her stomach, crying out in pain.

"Oh, no!" cried Sonya. "She's having one of her attacks. Please, someone get her some water."

Terri ran out of the store in search of water.

"Does she need a doctor?" asked a white-haired customer, who peered inquisitively at Angela's contorted face.

"No, she'll be fine once we get her some water," explained Sonya.

In all the commotion, the salesclerk, a sweet-looking, older woman, came running over. Angela made horrible gagging sounds as Terri appeared with a cup of water. She pretended only to be able to take a few drops. Then she started gagging again.

The saleswoman took Terri aside. "Are you sure your friend's all right? Should we call an ambulance or something? She sounds awful."

"She'll be okay," Terri assured her. "She has medication at home. We just have to get her out of here—fast."

Hurriedly, the woman gave Terri Sonya's purchase. "Next

time you're in the store, you can pay for the other tube, dear,'' she added.

Sonya and Dawn dragged their spluttering friend out of the store and then walked a safe distance from the entrance before bursting into laughter. Angela collapsed on a wooden bench, looking as though she'd gone into the second stage of her affliction.

"Boy, we just barely made it out of there," said Dawn. "Angela, you were brilliant."

"You think so?" Angela cried delightedly. "We still have to pay for the spilled glitter. I'll do it next week. I promise. That lady seemed really nice, but I wonder what would have happened if she'd said we *had* to pay right now."

"I don't know and I don't want to know," Sonya replied. "I'll give you some of the money, though."

"Me, too," said Terri.

"Me, too," said Dawn, even though none of them could figure out how to divide seventy four ways.

From the mall, they went to Terri's house. Terri's bedroom walls were covered with posters of gymnasts. Two small trophies sat on her dresser, along with a photograph of her gymnastics team.

The girls spread newspapers over the floor and then sprinkled glitter all over themselves: on their faces and arms and legs and of course in their hair.

"I bet you didn't have this much fun at Celia's," said Terri.

"Actually, I did," Sonya admitted. "We put tinfoil on our heads and cucumbers on our eyes."

The others stopped what they were doing and looked at Sonya as if she were crazy. Even after she explained what the cucumbers and tinfoil were for, they seemed skeptical.

"Sounds dumb," Terri said, wrinkling her nose. "I'm sure this is more fun."

"Hey, we can be the glitter sisters!" announced Angela.

"I know! Instead of stabbing ourselves with pins and being blood sisters like we did in third grade, let's be glitter sisters," suggested Dawn.

"That's a super idea," said Sonya. "We'll be shinier than the shiniest."

"We'll be the first ones at school to wear body glitter," added Angela.

"*And,*" Terri said with a smug smile, "everybody will look at us instead of at Celia, because we'll be wearing more glitter, and *we* will look totally cool."

Sonya didn't like the sound of that, but she kept her mouth shut, because the idea of looking totally cool was very exciting.

Nobody counted on the fact that after a while the glitter began to itch and besides, it washed off. Still, they planned to wear it to school on Monday. Afterward, Sonya thought that maybe being blood sisters was better than being glitter sisters because you couldn't ever wash that away. Your blood was combined with your friends' blood forever; there was no way to unmix it, and you would have to stay friends no matter what. Sonya wished there was a guarantee of staying friends like that—especially considering what happened next.

Chapter Six

✿

What happened next started on Monday morning when Sonya, Dawn, Terri, and Angela sprinkled glitter all over themselves and went to school. From the moment she arrived, Sonya felt dumb.

"Are you masquerading as a Christmas tree?" Howard Tarter asked her before class. She could tell he was ready to burst out laughing. And Howard didn't do much laughing. He usually just made other people laugh.

"I am trying to make a point," she said huffily, although she wasn't at all sure what that point was.

"You don't need glitter, Sonya," Howard informed her, and he walked away.

Sonya didn't know what he meant. She thought about it on the way to the restroom, where she washed all the glitter off. "You don't need glitter to be shiny?" she thought. "You don't need glitter to make a point?'' Maybe that was what he'd meant.

Still puzzled, Sonya went to her homeroom, and of course Terri said in a loud voice, ''Where's your glitter?''

''I took it all off. It—it was itching.'' Sonya glanced across the room and saw Celia with her gold-glittered hair, looking as pretty as always. Polly and Jeannie were wearing glitter in their hair, too, although they didn't look nearly as spectacular as Celia did. However, Sonya's friends looked like Christmas trees, just like Howard had said. What a dumb thing to do!

Terri, Dawn, and Angela kept glaring at Sonya during homeroom, but she couldn't talk to them until lunchtime. Why were they mad? Just because she'd rinsed off her glitter?

''Why didn't you tell us?'' Dawn demanded as soon as they sat down in the cafeteria.

''Tell you what?'' Sonya shot back.

''That Celia's friends were going to be glitter sisters, too!'' cried Angela.

Angrily, Sonya stuck her hands on her hips. ''Now how would I know that, Angela?''

''Because you're such good friends with Celia,'' Angela insisted. ''And you're supposed to be our spy.''

''I didn't know anything about it,'' Sonya replied, but her three friends looked at her as if they didn't believe her. ''Well, I didn't!'' she repeated. ''Do you think I would've thought up the glitter idea if I knew this?''

''Sure. Otherwise you would have worn your glitter today, too. But you didn't want us to look like we were copying Celia and her friends,'' said Terri. ''You're a traitor, Sonya.''

"That's not true!"

"It is too!"

Tears welled up in Sonya's eyes as she watched her three friends get up and flounce off to another table. She had no intention of following them, since she was sure they wouldn't talk to her, so she was glad when Celia asked her to eat with her.

"The thing about your friends is that they are so immature," said Celia.

Sonya nodded miserably. She sat through lunch watching her friends at the other table. It seemed as if they sat even closer than usual, as though they were closing out Sonya. Well, she would fix everything. She would give them a chance to do something fun, something they couldn't resist. She was going to ask Terri, Dawn, and Angela to come out to the ranch and ride horses after school. They'd like that. She'd ask Celia, too. Then her friends could see for themselves that Celia was just a nice, normal person.

"You have horses?" Celia's eyes lit up at Sonya's invitation.

"Yes. We live on a ranch," explained Sonya.

"I want to come, too," said Jeannie.

Polly propped up her big glasses. "I'm allergic to horses."

"Oh, I love them," said Celia, tossing her hair back. Eddie glided by and made a playful grab for her hair. Celia pulled away like a busy person who had no time to waste on such trivial matters.

The lunch period was almost over. Sonya dumped her tray

in the garbage and approached her friends' table. Immediately they stopped talking.

"Um, I thought you guys might like to come over after school and ride," she said.

"Oh, we'd love to!" Dawn exclaimed.

But Terri crossed her arms over her chest and stuck out her lower lip. "We'd love to if Celia's not going," she said pointedly.

"Well, I did invite her and Jeannie," Sonya admitted. "You don't have to talk to her or anything . . . Hey, you could do some spying!" Sonya didn't care how Celia and her friends got together, just as long as it happened. She was sure they could learn to like each other.

"I'm not going and that's final," said Terri. When Terri made up her mind, there was no budging her. She was like a rock. The other two girls didn't say anything.

"Are you coming?" Sonya asked them.

Dawn and Angela looked at each other. "I don't know," they both said sheepishly.

They're coming, Sonya told herself. I know they're coming. They just don't want to say so in front of Terri.

Sonya rushed home early to get the horses ready. Which ones should she choose? It depended on how well the girls rode. She decided to consult Bob.

Bob was chewing on a piece of straw, which caused him to whistle through his teeth as he answered her. "Well, I'll tell you, Sonya B. The roan, Freckles, is a nice horse, quiet and well-behaved. Amigo, the horse you've been riding, is a little more spirited. Then there's Flare. He runs nice, that one.''

"I'll let Celia and Dawn take turns on Flare," Sonya decided. "And Jeannie and Angela can share Freckles."

"I'll cinch them up for you, if you like," said Bob, pulling at the brim of his Stetson.

"I'll help you," said Sonya.

They started with Freckles.

"Now this horse bloats himself when you cinch him up," said Bob, "so that when he lets out his air, the cinch is loose. You cinch him, then you leave him for about five minutes and check the girth. He can't hold his breath for any longer'n that. Got it?''

"Yup," replied Sonya.

They went on to Flare, a small, spirited sorrel.

"This one doesn't like the bit, so you have to pry his mouth open, like this, and hold the top of the bridle between his ears, see?" The horse resisted the bit just as Bob said he would, but Bob put the bridle on in seconds, talking to the horse the whole time.

"Now Amigo is all yours. He doesn't complain about anything. Got the best nature of anybody around here." Bob grinned at her.

"Thanks," said Sonya.

"Any time." Bob slapped the horse's behind and wandered off toward the cow barn.

Sonya watched him go. She still thought he was kind of corny, but (she hated to admit this) he wasn't all that bad.

Celia arrived wearing riding boots and a new pair of jeans.

Jeannie looked fairly ordinary, although both girls were still wearing glitter. Sonya wished she had changed into a fancier pair of jeans, but there was no time for that now.

Celia turned out to be a natural on horseback. "These horses are great, Sonya," she exclaimed, as Flare walked around the ring. "Are they yours?"

"My stepfather's. He's a rancher," Sonya explained. "He owns all this property."

"Really? You're lucky."

Wally, the man hired to work around the stables, helped the girls with the horses. Once they were all settled on horseback, Celia and Jeannie followed Sonya along the trail that surrounded the ranch. Sonya kept checking over her shoulder, glancing at the drive to see if Angela or Dawn had arrived. At last she gave up. She couldn't believe they hadn't come.

"What are you looking for, Sonya?" Celia called.

"Oh, nothing," answered Sonya, feeling disappointed.

To hide her anger, she burst out laughing and changed the subject. "You know what?" she said to Celia and Jeannie. "Bob's a real scream. He looks like a cowboy on TV, and he talks like one, too." She imitated Bob's drawl.

The girls laughed.

"And he makes a big deal out of the fact that he fixes the best barbecue this side of the Mississippi," Sonya added. The others laughed again. Sonya realized Cowboy Bob really was pretty funny. She hadn't noticed it before. It was something to think about.

When the girls finished their ride and returned to the ranch, Bob was waiting for them. Sonya introduced her new friends.

"Y'all look too pretty to be out riding," he said, helping Celia dismount. Jeannie scrambled down from her horse on the wrong side and nearly fell on her face.

"You okay?" Sonya asked her.

"I'm fine," Jeannie said, dusting herself off.

"Next time, wear regular riding britches," suggested Bob. "Y'all come back now."

Celia giggled. "We will." She turned to Sonya. "This was really fun, Sonya. We'll have to do it again."

"We will." Sonya smiled, watching Bob amble off toward the barn. "Y'all come back now."

Celia and Jeannie walked to the gate, laughing.

Sonya looked around. Bob was unsaddling the horses. A group of ducks waddled down to the pond, and somewhere far off she heard a cow mooing. The ranch wasn't all that bad; in fact, Sonya was beginning to think it was pretty great.

But she couldn't help feeling that it would be a whole lot better with Terri, Dawn, and Angela around.

Chapter Seven

The next day was a school holiday and Sonya volunteered to go to the grocery store with her mother. She wanted to make sure her mom chose "good food," and the only way to do that was to push the cart and watch what went into it. Besides, apart from cleaning her room, Sonya didn't have anything better to do.

Sonya was surprised to find that her mom still took forever to shop. She compared all the prices, and slowly chose the biggest bargains. The meat counter was the worst. Sonya's mother paced in front of it, shaking her head, until she made a decision.

"Why do you even write a list?" Sonya wanted to know. "You don't buy half the stuff on it."

"I have to have a list," her mother insisted. She glanced

down in the basket at the Crunchy Munchies that Sonya had picked out. "Did I say you could have those?"

"No. Can I have those?" Sonya asked sweetly.

"Yes, but don't put anything else in the basket without my approval."

At the checkout stand, Sonya's mother met a friend of hers, Lilli Beasley, whom she hadn't seen in a year. Sonya picked up a copy of *The National Weekly News* and hid her face in it while the two women talked.

"I didn't even recognize you. You've changed so much, Nellie!" Mrs. Beasley exclaimed. She was carrying a baby in a Snugli pack on her front. The baby was asleep and its head flopped around as though it were a rag doll. "Did you do something to your hair?" Mrs. Beasley asked, still trying to figure out what was different about Sonya's mother.

She's turned into a cowgirl, thought Sonya. That's why you didn't recognize her.

"And Sonya, you've certainly grown up. Doesn't she look grown up, Nellie?"

"Yes, she does," Sonya's mother agreed, smiling proudly at Sonya.

Sonya hated it when her mother acted like this.

"I heard you got married, too," Mrs. Beasley went on.

"Yes, just this year. We have a ranch outside town," Sonya's mother explained.

"Oh, that's right. You married Bob Stretch," Mrs. Beasley exclaimed. "Now I remember. I went to high school with him."

"Oh, really?" Sonya's mother perked up.

Sonya sighed heavily. This conversation could go on for-ever. She read the headlines: "Pollution Can Make You Live Longer," "I Was A Test Tube Baby," "Pocahontas Finally Found."

She was just about to launch into the Pocahontas article when Mrs. Beasley's baby started to cry. Its wrinkled little face turned bright red and its toothless mouth formed a per-fect O. Sonya watched in fascination as the two women bent over the baby.

But she also made an interesting observation. She realized that both her mother and Mrs. Beasley had changed. And they were still friends. Sonya supposed that people were always changing but that that didn't make them better or worse—just different. So, she decided, maybe there's hope for the glitter sisters after all!

Finally, they reached the checker. Sonya put her newspaper on top of the groceries while her mother wasn't looking. The checker stuck the paper in the side of one of the bags, so that her mother only noticed it while wheeling the cart out of the store.

"Sonya, I didn't say you could buy this," she cried, yank-ing the paper out of the bag. "Such junk! Why do you read these papers?"

"I like them," Sonya said defensively. Sometimes her mom could be such a pain!

At school the next day Ms. Bell, looking pleased with her-self, wrote on the blackboard in large, exciting letters: DRA-MATIC ARTS.

"We're doing something a little different today, class," she announced. She appointed Sonya to pass out mimeographed sheets. "In order to begin our study of drama, we're going to perform a short skit about George Washington's courtship with Martha Custis. Now at that time, George was the best-known young man in Virginia. He was the defender of the colonists against the Indians and commander-in-chief of the Virginia forces. Martha was a widow with two children . . ."

Ms. Bell went on and on. Sonya perked up when she heard this: "And let's have Celia Forester play Martha, and Tommy Atwood play George."

It figures, thought Sonya. Tommy Atwood was the cutest boy in the sixth grade. He and Celia were a natural couple.

Howard Tarter let out a low whistle, like a birdcall.

"They meet at a dinner party, and shortly afterward make marriage plans," Ms. Bell explained, ignoring Howard. "George was supposed to be in Williamsburg getting ready for a battle when he met her, so let's imagine that scene."

The class was told to close their eyes and imagine George and Martha. The Washingtons seemed like a most unromantic couple to Sonya. She thought of George chopping down cherry trees, or at Valley Forge wearing rags. She knew almost nothing about Martha. Women didn't seem to get to say much in those days.

After Tommy and Celia had studied their lines on the mimeographed sheet, they stood in the front of the classroom.

"A pleasure to meet you, sir," said Celia, or Martha, curtseying stiffly.

Tommy turned beet red. "The pleasure is mine, Mrs. Custis,'' he read. ''As you know, I have military duties in Williamsburg, but I should like to see you again.''

Howard snorted loudly and made a whinnying, horselike sound.

''Howard, please be quiet,'' Ms. Bell ordered.

''I live very near Williamsburg, Mr. Washington,'' said Celia, batting her eyelashes. She managed to adopt a Southern accent for the occasion.

Howard raised his hand. ''George Washington hasn't got time for dessert, Ms. Bell, let alone all this conversation.''

''Howard, *please*. If you have something to offer the class, save it until we're finished.''

By now Tommy was completely flustered. Anybody would think he really was Washington and in a hurry to get somewhere. He shuffled from one foot to the other, and read his lines too quickly. Then, abruptly, he fell silent.

''Come *on*, Tommy,'' urged Celia.

A sputter of giggles erupted from the class. Tommy was supposed to kiss Celia's hand. Howard helpfully made chimpanzee noises and the students laughed loudly.

''Howard, I warned you before about those animalistic noises. Now if that's all you learned in Africa, which I'm sure it isn't . . .'' The teacher blushed, and Sonya wondered if she was remembering the naked statues. Ms. Bell sighed, then continued, ''Class, please allow George and Martha to complete their scene.''

Tommy opened his mouth to speak but no words came out. Celia nudged him, and daintily held out her hand. Finally,

Tommy kissed her hand. Then he backed away as if it were poison. The class whooped with laughter.

"Class, it is *not* that funny," Ms. Bell shouted in exasperation.

But, of course, it was that funny. Celia didn't laugh, though, and when Sonya looked around the room, she noticed that neither Jeannie nor Polly was laughing, either. Celia was acting rather elegant, in fact. She was a great actress. Sonya decided that was the mature way to be.

When the class finally quieted down, Ms. Bell assigned Sonya to narrate the ending of the skit.

"Fort Duquesne was taken, the war ended, and peace was restored," Sonya read carefully. "On January sixth, seventeen fifty-nine, George Washington and Martha Custis were married at her home."

The class clapped, and the bell rang. Sonya thought Ms. Bell looked relieved.

Howard walked out with Sonya.

"Why didn't you laugh?" he asked her. "That was the funniest class we've had yet. And those were some of my best chimp imitations."

"Sorry, Howard. I didn't mean to disappoint you," said Sonya.

"What I go through to entertain you," he moaned.

"What's going on?" asked Angela, as she, Terri, and Dawn met Sonya and Howard in the hall.

"You should have seen how Tommy kissed Celia's hand," Howard said, grinning. "Like she was a cactus."

"Howard made him nervous," Sonya said. "Wouldn't you be nervous?"

Dawn and Angela stopped in their tracks. "What's wrong with you, Sonya? How come you're not laughing or anything? It's like you're a brainwashed person."

"That's right," Terri agreed. "Sonya, Celia has brainwashed you into a stuck-up person."

"She has not! I'm still the same. I am *not* stuck-up," Sonya cried out.

"You are, too," Angela chimed in.

"Am not."

"Are, too." Terri stood with her hands on her hips.

"Well, you know what you are, don't you?" Sonya quivered with unshed tears.

"No, what?" Terri pushed her face up close to Sonya's.

"You're jealous and immature!" There. She'd said it. The accusation dangled in the silence, while her three friends shook their heads. "We'll see who's immature around here, Miss Stuck-Up."

Sonya gulped back tears. Her three friends—no, her three *ex*-friends—marched off down the hall.

At lunch, Sonya sat with Celia and pretended not to notice her friends. But she looked at them every time she thought they weren't looking at her. She saw that Terri was too loud, too bossy, and too mean. And she saw that Dawn was too babyish, a marshmallow who believed anything anybody told her. All Angela thought about was food. How could a mature person have friends like that?

For the first time since she'd been at Gladstone, Sonya biked all the way home alone. Halfway there, it began to rain. By the time she reached the door, she was sopping wet.

On the front doorstep she found a stack of records—all rain-soaked. They were hers! She had lent them to Terri a week ago. A note was attached: "Sonya—these have cooties. Terri."

Sonya stood on the doorstep in shock. Rain dripped off her nose and splashed onto the wet records. She didn't know how Terri had beaten her to the ranch, but she didn't care. Terri could be mean, but Sonya had never known her to be *this* mean! And not to her! Leaving her records out in the rain! How could she do that? What had gotten into her?

The worst was yet to come. Celia Forester phoned.

"Guess what? I got an audition for a sit-com," Celia sang into the phone.

"Oh, that's great, Celia," Sonya said, glad somebody was happy. "When is it?"

"In a couple of weeks. I'll have to practice my lines every day, but Barb says I have a good chance of getting the part."

"I'm really happy for you."

"Oh, and Sonya, I didn't want to tell you this, but"—she paused for emphasis—"I was in the girls' room after lunch today and I heard Terri talking to Angela. They think you've become a snob since you lived in New York. They say you're trying to be better than everyone else, and they don't want to be friends with you anymore."

Sonya bit her lip. Act casual, she told herself. Act like you don't care. "Oh, really?" was all she said.

"I just thought you should know," Celia added quickly. "*I* don't think that at all. They're just jealous because we're friends now."

Sonya felt as if somebody had socked her in the stomach. And she hadn't felt that way in a long time. Not since Angela threw a baseball and it really had hit her there. Celia must be right, thought Sonya, even though she didn't want to believe it. But all the evidence was staring her in the face: Terri returning the records and leaving them in the rain, the way her friends had acted lately. They weren't being true friends at all.

"Yeah," she said finally, but it hurt to say so. "I think you're right."

Chapter Eight

Sonya's eleventh birthday was in three weeks. Usually she was so excited she counted the days, constantly reminding everybody of the latest figure. "Guess what, ten more shopping days until my birthday," she'd say again and again. But this year she was just plain nervous. She was practically new to Gladstone, her friends had abandoned her—yet, somehow, she still wanted her party to be fabulous.

Sonya sat at the kitchen table, writing a guest list. Maybe she should invite boys to her birthday party as well. Howard Tarter would be fun to have around. He could make animalistic noises and fit right in with the livestock at the ranch.

Sonya's list read like this:

> Celia Forester
> Jeannie Sandlin

Polly Clinker
Howard Tarter?

On second thought, she couldn't invite just one boy because he'd feel weird with all those girls. What about Tommy Atwood?

Her mom peered over her shoulder. "What about Terri, Dawn, and Angela? Aren't you inviting them?" she asked.

"They don't get along with my new friends, Mom," Sonya said.

"Did you have a fight or something? I haven't seen them around for a couple of days."

"No, nothing like that." Sonya bit her lip. She didn't like to discuss personal things with her mother. Her mom would start making all sorts of suggestions which Sonya wouldn't want to follow.

"But they're your *best* friends, Sonya," her mother said. "You can't exclude them. It's not fair. Put them on the list and we'll send out invitations."

"Your mother's right, Sonya," said Bob. "Friends aren't that easy to come by. Better take care of 'em."

Sonya's mother beamed at him as though he'd said something brilliant. Sonya did as she was told, but she didn't feel good about it. Terri wouldn't come, and Angela and Dawn would do whatever Terri did.

Suddenly, Sonya wished she knew what was going on with them. The house was too quiet. She was used to their calling and coming by. She hated knowing that they were making plans without her. Sonya liked Celia, but Celia was always busy after school now that she was rehearsing for the audition. Why couldn't her old and new friends get along?

One day Ms. Bell announced that she was giving a big English test on the following Monday. Sonya went home every day after school to study. It gave her something to do. And she had a feeling Ms. Bell's tests could be tough.

"I don't need to study much for that thing," said Celia confidently as they were leaving the classroom on Friday. "Besides, I've got to get ready for the audition. Do you want to go to the mall and help me pick out something to wear?"

"No, thanks. I've got to study," said Sonya, wishing she could go shopping. Too bad she didn't feel as confident about the test as Celia did.

On Sunday, Mrs. Forester drove Celia over to the ranch, and Celia ran into Sonya's room, breathlessly excited. "Listen," she exclaimed. "Close the door so your parents won't hear."

Sonya did as she was told.

Celia flounced down on the bed. "I've got a great idea. I haven't studied for the test at all. You know how important this audition is to me. And I know you studied. So let me copy your test paper. We sit across the aisle from each other, and it would be so easy—"

"I can't do that!" protested Sonya. "What if we get caught?"

"We won't." Celia lowered her voice conspiratorially. "Ms. Bell thinks I'm an angel. Look, if you let me copy your test, I'll get you an audition for the show I'm trying out for. I promise.''

"Really?'' The idea was exciting. Sonya could go down in history. She could be as glamorous as Celia. She could actually be on TV. Wow!

But this was dangerous. Sonya didn't know what to do. Her old friends weren't her friends anymore, and she needed them. All the good things seemed to happen to Celia. *She* got the audition, *she* was the star of the skit, *she* got all the attention, just like Terri said. Could Celia's luck rub off on me? Sonya asked herself. She wasn't sure. And Ms. Bell might think Celia was an angel, but what did she think of Sonya?

"I don't know . . .'' said Sonya hesitantly.

"I promise, Sonya,'' Celia repeated, looking her straight in the eye. "It'll work perfectly.''

Sonya had heard that people couldn't lie when they looked you straight in the eye. She gulped. Even if that were true, she was still scared. "Okay,'' she agreed in a small voice. But she felt awful.

"Thanks, Sonya,'' Celia said. "Listen, I have to go. My mom's waiting for me in the car.'' And with that, Celia ran out of Sonya's room and all the way to Mrs. Forester's car.

"What's her hurry?'' asked Cowboy Bob as he was nearly knocked over by Celia.

"She's got to watch her sister on TV. Big event,'' said Sonya, figuring that was as good a story as any.

"We've got TVs here, Sonya. With different-sized screens.''

"We've got it all," added her mother.

Sonya had forgotten about the TVs. Big deal. Who cared? Sonya had bigger problems today. She had become a liar, and tomorrow she would be a cheat, too. Already launched on a life of crime—at the age of eleven! And her parents didn't even know it!

Chapter Nine

The night before the test, Sonya could barely study. Her brain felt like watered-down oatmeal. She couldn't sleep, either. Her mom and Bob were up watching a late movie, and she wished they'd go to bed so she could sneak into the kitchen and raid the refrigerator. When she was this nervous (and she wasn't sure she'd ever been this nervous before), all she wanted to do was stuff her face.

Sonya's mother and Bob didn't go to bed until eleven o'clock. At a quarter past eleven, Sonya tiptoed to the kitchen and made a peanut-butter sandwich. Then she brushed her hair fifty times to make it shine like Barbara Forester's, and crawled into bed.

Sleep was weird, Sonya reflected as she lay there with her eyes open. When you wanted to stay awake for something, like a good movie, you almost always fell asleep. When you needed your sleep because of a test, you turned into a raving insomniac.

She reread some *National Weekly News* articles, turned out the light, and lay staring at the ceiling. When she woke in the morning, she didn't feel as if she had slept at all.

She didn't eat breakfast, either.

"Are you sick, Sonya?" her mother asked.

"No, just on a diet," she replied. She was getting good at this lying business.

"Breakfast is the most important meal of the day, right?" her mother said, looking anxiously at Bob.

He peered over the rim of the newspaper. "That's right, Nellie. Sonya, eat your Toasties, as they say on TV."

Sonya rolled her eyes. She shook a few flakes into a cereal bowl, just to pacify them. As soon as they left for work, she poured the cereal back into the box.

Suddenly, Sonya knew she couldn't go through with Celia's plan. Celia would have to take the test without her help. She phoned the Foresters.

"I'm just leaving," Celia cried breathlessly when she'd picked up the phone.

"Don't do it, Celia," Sonya warned. "I know you'll be sorry."

"Oh, don't be such a scaredy-cat," Celia said lightly. "Just write the answers on the desk or something. No big deal."

"No, I won't," Sonya said.

"C'mon, Sonya, you can't back out on me. I mean, what are friends for?"

"I won't do it," insisted Sonya, but she had the feeling that Celia hadn't heard a word she'd said.

When Sonya entered her English class that morning, Celia was already sitting at her desk, smiling her angelic smile at Ms. Bell. No problem, thought Sonya, but her stomach was twisted into a bunch of knots. Celia turned her smile on Sonya, and Sonya found that she couldn't smile back. Ms. Bell passed out the test papers, then recited the instructions, which included the phrase, "Keep your eyes on your own paper."

The test began. Ms. Bell paced around the room, always watching. Sonya broke out in a cold sweat. There was no way to write on her desk without being observed. There was no way to write anywhere except on the test paper. Ms. Bell had eagle eyes. Celia must have been crazy even to think of cheating in Ms. Bell's room.

Five minutes into the test, Celia hissed at her. Sonya froze. She couldn't respond. Celia would hate her, but she had to take that chance.

Sonya was not going to cheat.

But Celia wasn't going to give up. She leaned over and squinted at Sonya's paper. Sonya's arm was crooked around it, and she didn't move. She didn't dare look up. She didn't dare move a muscle. A moment later, she heard Celia's pencil scratching on her paper, stopping, and then a movement as she leaned over again.

Click, click, click.

Sonya jumped when she heard Ms. Bell's high-heeled shoes as the teacher strode purposefully down the aisle. Sonya's vision blurred. She was dizzy. She was in trouble. Celia was perfect—nothing would happen to her. . . .

"Celia, may I have your paper, please?" asked Ms. Bell in a cold, polite tone.

"My paper?"

Every head in the class jerked up to see what was going on. Celia smiled innocently at Ms. Bell, but the teacher didn't return the smile. And Sonya saw that Celia's hand trembled as she handed over the paper.

"Thank you, Celia. See me after class," said Ms. Bell.

"But I don't understand why."

"This is not something we want to discuss in front of the class, Celia." Ms. Bell's voice was icy. The teacher turned on her heel and deposited the paper on her desk.

Everyone exchanged looks but no one said anything. Just before the bell rang, Ms. Bell collected the rest of the test papers. When most of the students had filed out of the class, Celia made her way to the front of the room. Sonya was the last one to leave, and she heard muffled voices after she had closed the door.

"Ms. Bell, why didn't you let me finish my test?" Celia asked.

"You know very well why," said Ms. Bell. "You were cheating, young lady. You were copying from Sonya Plummer's paper."

"But I wasn't!" Celia cried. "You must have been seeing things! *Sonya* was the cheater!"

Sonya couldn't believe her ears. Had she really heard Celia say that?

Ms. Bell replied crossly, "I am not blind, Celia. And don't lie to me. I saw you with my own eyes. And I'm surprised at you. You're usually a good student."

"It's not fair!" cried Celia.

Sonya heard footsteps coming toward the closed door, so she bolted down the hall and hid in the stairwell. A second later, Celia flung the door to the classroom open and stormed out. She didn't look to either side, just walked straight ahead, and passed Sonya without seeming to see her.

"Celia!" Sonya ran after her. "Celia, I'm sorry about what happened. I tried to tell you . . . but you wouldn't listen. Um, I hope you didn't get in trouble," she went on nervously.

Celia stopped long enough to glare at her. "It's all your fault, Sonya. You're the one who should be in trouble, not me. I never want to speak to you again."

Celia left Sonya standing in the hallway by herself. Jeannie Sandlin approached her. "Hey, listen, Sonya," she said. "Celia has never been in trouble in school before. She's always been perfect. Now she feels like she has to put the blame on someone."

"What are you, a junior psychologist?" Sonya asked bitterly. She swallowed hard to keep from crying.

"Well, I know her pretty well," replied Jeannie. "She's my friend, but she can be a creep sometimes."

"She was supposed to be *my* friend, too, Jeannie."

Sonya hurried away. She went into the lunchroom and looked for her ex-friends. They were horsing around at the counter, arguing with Eddie and Howard.

Sonya picked out her food and followed her ex-friends to

their table. When Terri noticed her, she frowned. "What're you doing here?" she asked.

"I want to talk to you."

"Go ahead."

"Do you still think I'm a snob?" Sonya asked.

Dawn's face crumpled as though she were going to cry.

Terri glared at Sonya. "Yes, we still think you're a snob. And worse."

"Worse?"

"Yes. We heard you're also a cheat."

"A cheat? That's not true!" cried Sonya. "Who said that?"

Angela and Dawn looked sympathetically at Sonya, but they didn't argue with Terri. Nobody argued with Terri, unless it was absolutely necessary.

Sonya's tears were ready to burst out now and make an idiot of her. She gripped her lunch tray with both hands, accidentally pressing her fingers deep into her tuna-fish sandwich. "I thought *you* guys would believe me, even if we're not friends anymore."

Sonya stomped away, leaving the tray on a table. She had to get out of there—before someone saw her cry.

In gym class, Howard Tarter walked around Sonya, sniffing.

"Howard, what're you doing?" she asked him.

"I wasn't sure it was you. I mean, it's not like you," he said, still sniffing.

"What's not like me?" she demanded.

"I hate to tell you this, Sonya, but you smell like tuna fish." He grinned.

"Oh, great." Sonya sniffed her fingers. Sure enough, Howard was right. She turned to him, annoyed. "Who are you, Sherlock Holmes?"

He shrugged. "As I said, it's not like you. Just thought you'd want to know, that's all."

"Gee, thanks, Howie," said Sonya sarcastically.

"Look, if I didn't warn you, packs of cats might follow you home from school."

Sonya groaned. "I'll wash my hands right now." Sometimes Howard, for all his worldly knowledge and brains, could be so immature.

Still, Sonya wondered if Howard might be a true friend. What was a true friend, anyway? Did a true friend tell you when you smelled like tuna fish, or if your shoe was untied? Did a true friend turn you in for cheating when you didn't cheat?

Sonya washed her hands and, while she was at it, her face. Then she ran out to the track, where the gym teacher, Ms. Patterson, was timing the students as they ran laps.

Groups of four runners were clocked together. Sonya got in position with three other students and waited for Ms. Patterson to shout, "Go!" Halfway into the first lap, Sonya passed Angela, Terri, and Dawn. When they saw her, they made faces at her but didn't say anything. It didn't seem possible that they were the same girls she'd gone shopping with a few days before. They didn't look capable of having a good time.

Then she passed Celia, Polly, and Jeannie. Celia tossed her hair and pretended not to notice her, Polly copied Celia, and Jeannie gave her a wavery smile. Sonya remembered what Celia had looked like wearing cucumbers and tinfoil. How could Celia be that much fun and act like such a snob, too? It was hard to feel sorry for her. In fact, it was hard to like her at all now.

Sonya ran on, passing Howard, who made animalistic noises at her. She would have laughed at him except that her life was a mess. She didn't even have a true friend anymore— unless you counted Howard.

And Sonya didn't know whether she could count a boy.

Chapter Ten

When Sonya got home from school, a letter from her father was waiting. She snatched it off the counter and took it to her room along with a handful of chocolate-chip cookies. In her opinion, the best thing to do when miserable was eat and lie around in her room with the stereo blasting. She couldn't stand for anyone to see her cry, because she was fair-skinned, and her face became blotchy. Sonya glanced in the mirror and said, "I am the ugliest person in the world when I cry, so just don't let me do it."

Then she went over to her bed and lay down and read her father's letter:

Dear Sonya,
  I miss you. I imagine you're enjoying the new ranch and school. I know it's an adjustment after N.Y., but I

remember how you missed your friends when you first moved here.

Things are good. Went to a play the other night with Edress, the woman you called the Snowy Egret because she's so tall and elegant.

How about coming home for Christmas? Love to have you. Think it over.

Love,
Dad

He wanted her to come "home" for Christmas. Well, it was nice to be wanted. Imagine, Sonya hadn't been able to wait to get back to Gladstone to be with her best friends, and had left some pretty decent friends behind in New York. When she had lived there, she had missed Angela, Terri, and Dawn dreadfully. In her imagination, they had been perfect—the best things since bubble ice cream. But maybe Sonya had made a mistake. Maybe the New York friends were better than she remembered. And maybe Christmas with her father wouldn't be such a bad idea.

Sonya tried to start her homework, but couldn't concentrate on it. She wandered into the den and switched on the TV, only to see Barbara's beautiful face and sparkly hair. She turned the set off.

Sonya wandered back to her room and stood in front of the mirror, brushing her hair until it shone. It wasn't any longer, but it was shiny. Maybe someday she *would* be a sensation like Barbara or Celia—except she would be a nicer person. She would be a real personality. Of course, she didn't know

Barbara at all. She only knew what she looked like. But if she acted anything like Celia, well . . .

"Yoo-hoo! Anybody home?"

Sonya's mom barged right into Sonya's room. Bob was behind her. They took one look at Sonya and knew something was wrong.

"Your hair's awful pretty, but you look like you had a fight with the whole world," Bob remarked.

"What happened, honey?" her mom asked, wrapping her arm around her shoulders.

Sonya hated sympathy when she was upset—it just made her more upset.

"Nothing," she said, biting her lip to keep back the tears.

But Sonya had forgotten that moms have built-in radar, so that kind of an answer was not sufficient. They almost always knew when a kid was trying to hide something.

"Tell me, honey. Is it your friends?" her mother persisted.

Suddenly Sonya couldn't stand it anymore and burst into tears. Bob snuck off to another room. When Sonya was able to speak again, she told her mother how Celia had cheated and then blamed her.

But surprisingly, her mother didn't say anything bad about Celia. She didn't jump on Sonya's side, either. She just said, "Let's have some tea. I bought this ranch-style brand I want you to try."

"Is everything ranch-style now?" Sonya asked, but she didn't really care.

"Oh, it's just the theme, honey. I love the ranch. I guess I'm going through a stage. You know, sometimes friends go through stages, too. They don't always want the same things at the same times.''

''Yes, but I thought I'd be best friends with Terri and Angela and Dawn forever.'' Sonya sniffed into a Kleenex.

''Maybe you will be. I'm best friends with Lilli, even though we fought like crazy sometimes and misunderstood each other.'' Sonya's mother began to look wistful then, as if she'd gone somewhere Sonya couldn't follow. ''We even fell for the same boy once.''

''Really? How old were you?''

''Thirteen.''

Sonya wondered if any of her friends liked Howard. He wasn't really their type, but then she didn't know what their type was.

''You have to figure that the four of you are going to grow at different rates,'' her mother said.

Sonya sighed. ''Mom, I get the picture. You don't have to go on and on.'' Because that was just what her mother would do—go on forever, once she got wound up.

Her mother went into the kitchen to make the tea, and Sonya found herself smiling. She actually felt a little better.

That week, Sonya didn't have anyone to talk to, except Howard. And Howard wasn't a big talker. Still, Sonya looked forward to whatever he did say because it was always interesting or funny.

Terri, Dawn, and Angela continued to snub her whenever they saw her. Celia did the same thing, except that she did it in a very sophisticated way, tossing her red hair as though she were either a horse or a famous actress. Sonya heard that Celia was going to fly to Hollywood a couple of days a week for the sake of her career, but Sonya didn't show any interest. Sometimes, she wished the plane would crash.

On Friday morning, Sonya was walking down the hall at school when she saw a big cluster of students. Terri's loud voice rose above the others, and then she saw Celia, Jeannie, and Polly yelling at her former best friends. Celia's face was beet red.

"Immature, immature, immature!" Celia was yelling. Several boys stood around, elbowing each other and laughing.

Curious, Sonya walked closer to them to see what was going on.

But before she reached them, a teacher strode toward the group. "All right, break it up. Time for class!" the teacher cried, shooing them along.

The kids grumbled as the group broke up.

"What happened?" Sonya asked Eddie, but he just shrugged.

"I don't really know," he said disappointedly. "I was hoping they'd pull each other's hair out or something." He ran to catch up with his friends.

Sonya wished she knew what the girls had been yelling about, but then she remembered that they weren't her friends anymore. Well, what did she care? Let them tear each other's hair out, she thought as she hurried down the hall.

Chapter Eleven

88

"I wish I'd cancelled the party," Sonya muttered miserably as she strung crepe-paper streamers around the gazebo next to the ranch house. "Nobody's going to come."

"Don't say that," her mother replied gently. "Your friends will show up, I'm sure."

Sonya felt like Dorothy in the Land of Oz. Me against the world, she thought. Nobody believes I'm right, so I don't have any friends.

It seemed like ages since Sonya had first set foot in Gladstone Elementary, but it had only been several weeks. She'd had such hopes for making this the best school year ever. So far, it hadn't turned out very well. Here it was her birthday—and she was scared nobody would even bother to show up!

"Sonya, I want you to open this package," Bob said, handing her a small box.

She set down the roll of crepe paper, accepted the box from Bob and tore off the wrapping. Sonya had never been reluctant about opening presents, no matter how depressed she was. Inside the box, a tiny gold charm in the shape of a star lay nestled against blue velvet. It was something she might have picked out for herself.

"I love it, Bob. Thanks," she blurted out, before she remembered she didn't like him all that much.

"I saw it in the window of a jewelry store, and I thought, that just looks like Sonya," he told her, grinning wide under the brim of his Stetson.

"It's perfect. Thanks," she said. She thought of leaning over and kissing him, but she wasn't ready for that yet. Besides, she didn't want to give him the idea that she was starting to like him.

A station wagon drew up outside the gate to the ranch and a couple of kids tumbled out, running like crazy toward the gazebo. Sonya recognized Bob's twin nieces, Heather and Holly. The two eight-year-olds thrust packages into Sonya's arms, then ran to Bob and hugged him. Sonya placed the packages on the redwood picnic table outside the gazebo.

"See? I told you somebody would come," her mother said happily.

"Oh, Mom. Relatives don't count," grumbled Sonya. She squinted longingly at the horizon, hoping *somebody* would show up. Just one friendly face would be enough. Or even an unfriendly one. Boy, am I getting desperate, she thought.

"Well, why don't I get the cake," her mother said brightly. She dashed into the house, with Holly and Heather in tow.

Half an hour later, the ice-cream cake was melting in the sun. Sonya scowled. She could no longer act as if she didn't care.

"Nobody's coming, Mom. I think we'd better put the cake away," she said softly.

"Nonsense. Why don't we play a game?" her mother suggested.

Sonya heaved a sigh. "I'm really tired of everybody pretending nothing's wrong. I'm not six years old, Mom. What do you suggest? Tiddlywinks?" Parents could be so dumb sometimes.

"Look, lots of people get the birthday blues, Sonya," Bob said.

"How many people give a birthday party which nobody shows up for?" she asked. Then she pointed to the melting cake. "Do you want a great big puddle out here, Mom?"

"Maybe we should put it away—just until the guests arrive," her mother replied.

Sonya's throat tightened. This was the worst birthday of her life. And everybody was being extra-specially nice to her, which made it worse than the worst. The Great Eleventh Birthday Disaster, Sonya thought. This could make headlines, except that she sure didn't want anyone to know about it.

Just then, they heard a familiar shout.

"Hey, Stuck-up! Happy birthday!"

Sonya whirled around in time to see Terri's mother's car pulling to a stop at the gate. Terri and Sonya's two other ex-friends burst out of the car and raced toward her.

Sonya had never been so happy to see anyone in her entire life.

"I thought you weren't coming," she exclaimed. "I thought we weren't friends anymore."

Dawn immediately began to cry.

"Do you think we could miss your birthday party?" she asked tearfully. "Well, actually, we couldn't decide if you really wanted us here. I mean, after what we said the other day."

"I didn't think we'd ever talk to each other again," Sonya admitted.

"Celia kept making up all this stuff about you," said Angela. "She said you thought you were better than everyone. And she said *you* were the cheater."

"But we never believed that, did we?" said Dawn to the others.

"But you were mad at me," Sonya reminded them. "How come?"

Of course, Sonya knew that her friends had sort of believed Celia, just as Sonya had sort of believed the things Celia had said about Terri, Angela, and Dawn. But she didn't want to think about all that now.

"Well, anyway, it's all settled," said Terri. "On Friday we got into a big fight with Celia in the hallway. Howard kept saying that Ms. Bell never even suspected you, but Celia insisted you had cheated. I noticed that even Jeannie and Polly weren't going along with her. And Celia was going on about how you thought we were jealous and immature and—"

"So that's what that fight was about!" Sonya remembered

Eddie wishing the girls would tear each other's hair out. And she smiled to think that Howard had been sticking up for her. "How'd the fight start?" she wanted to know.

Dawn told the story. "Terri was running down the hall carrying her lunch when she ran into Celia. Her thermos fell on the floor and milk splashed all over Celia's shoes. Celia accused Terri of doing it on purpose, Terri called her a snob—"

"And the rest is history," Terri finished up.

"Can we celebrate now?" Angela interrupted with a pained expression on her face.

"Oh, right! We should celebrate," Dawn exclaimed.

"Presents or cake first?" Terri asked.

"Cake!" cried Angela.

"Presents!" yelled everybody else.

Angela licked her lips and glanced around hungrily. Dawn leaned over and patted her hand.

"Angela, we'll open the presents in a hurry, then we can have cake, okay?" said Sonya.

Angela sighed. "Okay," she agreed reluctantly.

The four friends sat on the gazebo lawn chairs in a circle around Sonya. Sonya ripped the pink wrapping off of Dawn's present first, and revealed a pair of teddy bear earrings.

"Oh, these are so cute!" said Sonya, giving her friend a hug.

Then she opened Angela's present, which was heavy and clunky and turned out to be an elephant bank in the same colors as her bedroom.

"This is adorable, Angela. Thanks," Sonya said, feeling like a princess.

Terri's present was a pair of wildly striped socks. "For horseback riding," she explained.

"Oh, I love them. Thanks—thanks a lot, everybody," cried Sonya. Her feet were buried in wrapping paper and ribbons. "You can't believe how great it is to have a birthday after all. And best friends."

Everyone grinned except Angela. "Sonya, where's the cake?" she asked. "I thought you were going to have an ice-cream cake this year."

The girls laughed. Sonya said, "I'll get the cake." Happily, she went inside. The cake had refrozen into strange swirls of color, but it still tasted good. Sonya didn't care one bit what it looked like. She had her friends, and she had her party.

Right then, nothing else in the world mattered.

Chapter Twelve

It was great to go to school on Monday morning as a person with friends. Sonya looked around for Celia. She wanted to tell her off. But when she saw her all by herself on the playground, she decided to leave her alone. For once in Celia Forester's life, no one was paying any attention to her. Not even Polly Clinker and Jeannie Sandlin. The boys were on the front steps of the school, tossing a ball back and forth. Nobody was trying to pick glitter out of her hair. It seemed as if the entire sixth grade had lost interest in her.

Howard Tarter tugged at Sonya's sleeve. "Hey, I heard your party was great."

"Yeah, it was. Thanks." Sonya said. She hadn't invited Howard after all, because boys usually didn't want to come to girls' parties. Even mature boys like Howard. Besides, she was kind of embarrassed at the thought that Howard would know she liked him.

"How'd you find out about the party?" she asked.

"I heard everybody talking about it," he replied.

Sonya smiled. "Everybody" had to be Angela, Terri, and Dawn. Who else could spread that rumor?

Later that day, Sonya and Howard walked to English class together. Ms. Bell handed back the test papers. Sonya noticed that there was no paper on Celia's desk. The rest of the class noticed, too, and started whispering. Celia turned beet red. She tried to ignore everybody.

But Howard leaned over and asked innocently, "What did you get on the test, Celia?"

Celia didn't answer. A few kids laughed. Ms. Bell made them be quiet.

After class, Sonya saw Howard notice Celia in the hall and go over to talk to her.

"What'd she say?" Sonya asked as she walked toward her locker.

Howard shrugged. "Not much. I tried to amuse her with my elephant call but she wasn't interested."

"Try me, Howard," Sonya suggested.

Howard let out a bellow—really elephant-like. His face turned bright red with the effort. A teacher frowned at him and shook her finger warningly.

"Ms. Bell's going to love it, Howard," Sonya said. "I think it's your best animalistic noise."

Pleased, Howard walked away.

Sonya met her friends at their lockers. "Celia has been all alone today," she announced.

"I wonder what that means," said Dawn.

"It wouldn't mean anything if it was one of us," Terri said. "But Celia is *never* alone. She's not the alone type. Think about it."

"You're right," Sonya agreed. "She usually has admirers. But nobody except Howard went near her after class."

"Look, you guys," Angela said authoritatively. "Celia is all by herself because everyone in our class knows she tried to copy from Sonya's test paper."

"How do they know?" Sonya asked. "All they know is she didn't get a paper back. Last week they all believed *her*."

"They know because of the fight on Friday. The fight kind of announced it to the entire school," Terri said proudly. "At least I think that's what happened. See, I pointed out that Celia is Ms. Bell's pet, so Ms. Bell wouldn't accuse her of cheating without a good reason. I guess everyone really listened to me. And now all Celia's friends—and her enemies— are embarrassed by her."

"Nobody wants to hang around her," added Dawn.

"Wow, that's serious. Polly Clinker would be friends with anyone," said Angela.

A couple of days ago, Sonya would have been friends with anyone, too. "I know how Polly feels," she said. "Wanting to belong makes you do funny things."

"Ha, ha. You'd never find me *that* desperate," scoffed Terri.

"How do you know, Terri?" Sonya demanded.

"I just know it."

"I think we should form a new club," Sonya said. "I think we should renew our vows as blood sisters."

"I second the motion!" cried Dawn. The others chimed in.

"And everyone should know who we are," said Sonya. "We should be more visible."

"We could be the High Visibility Gang," suggested Terri.

"Or the Visibles," Dawn offered.

"And the deal is, we each have to do something really visible," said Sonya.

"Like take off all our clothes?" joked Terri.

"Not *that* visible," said Sonya.

"I'm going to try out for the lead in the school play," announced Angela.

After much thought, Dawn said, "I'll be lunch monitor this month."

The four burst into giggles.

Sonya had gotten an A on her English test. Celia, however, had gone home right after class that day. Howard said she went home sick. But Sonya wondered if Celia was really sick, or if she just couldn't take being alternately teased and ignored. Or maybe she hadn't liked Howard's elephant blast.

In Sonya's opinion, Celia had gotten herself into trouble, but she felt sorry for her because she was in so *much* trouble and because no one liked her anymore. And because she was in trouble at home, too. Her mom must be more disappointed in her than ever. Sonya didn't tell her friends that, because they wouldn't understand.

Sonya knew she'd never be friends with Celia again. Not after what Celia had done to her. Celia wasn't somebody you could call a true friend. A true friend was somebody who could make mistakes, or watch you make mistakes, and still come back and forgive you and understand. A true friend could also get away with telling you really gross things about yourself that nobody else would have the guts to say.

There was a strong possibility that Howard Tarter was a true friend, Sonya decided. And, of course, so were her best friends.

After school that day, the four friends went to Terri's house for the blood ceremony. Terri produced a needle and stuck everybody's fingers. Then they pressed their index fingers together until their blood was completely mixed.

"Now we all have Type A-B-negative-positive," said Sonya happily. "And nothing will ever keep us apart again, right?"

The others stopped sucking their punctured fingers long enough to answer loudly, "Right!"

About the Author

SUSAN SMITH was born in Great Britain and has lived most of her life in California. She began writing when she was thirteen years old and has authored a number of successful teenage novels, including the *Samantha Slade* series published by Archway Paperbacks. Currently, she lives in Brooklyn with her two children. Both children have provided her with many ideas and observations that she has included in her books. In addition to writing, Ms. Smith enjoys travel, horseback riding, skiing, and swimming.